Hearts and Hooves

PALACEPET243

Code is valid for your Whisker Haven ebook and may be redeemed through the Disney Story Central app on the App Store. Content subject to availability. Parent permission required.
Code expires on December 31, 2019.

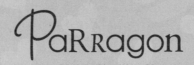

PaRragon

Bath · New York · Cologne · Melbourne · Delhi
Hong Kong · Shenzhen · Singapore

Colorful Cake-tillion

Berry needs help finishing her cake for Cake-tillion. Decorate the cake and then color it in!

2

Derby Dash

Petite is practicing for the Royal Derby. Guide her through the maze to the finish line. Be careful not to run into any obstacles or trample the flowers!

START

FINISH LINE

3

Answer on page 47

Whisker Woods

Whisker Woods is a great place to play hide and seek. Can you help Ms. Featherbon spot the pets and objects hiding in the picture below?

Dreamy

Treasure

Sultan

Can you find four beautiful butterflies, too?

Petite

Mushroom

Flower

Answers on page 47

Color in this picture of the royal friends cleaning the castle together.

Book Belle

Petite is looking for her books! Help her get through the maze and collect them along the way.

Start

Finish

Answer on page 47

Sweet Dreams

Catnap time! Help Dreamy get to her throne by following the right path.

a b c

Hint:
Dreamy's throne
is pink with
bows!

8

Answer on page 47

Cute Close-ups

Can you name the precious pets in these pictures?
Draw lines to match the close-ups to their owners.

a Berry

b Pumpkin

c Petite

d Treasure

9

Answers on page 47

Knight Night Guard

Sultan really wants to be the next Knight Night Guard! Connect the dots to see his special helmet.

Now add color!

4

5

3

2

6

9

8

7

10

1

11

13

12

Showtime!

There can't be a dance recital without Pumpkin! Help Ms. Featherbon find the star of the show using the key below.

Start

| Up | Down | Left | Right |

Answer on page 47

Finish

Follow the paw prints!

11

Beautiful Butterflies

Pumpkin loves chasing butterflies. How many red, yellow, blue and purple butterflies can you count in this picture? Write the answers in the boxes below.

Answers on page 47

Oh My Blueberry Pie!

Berry loves baking treats for her friends. Look carefully at this picture of her kitchen for 30 seconds, then cover it with a piece of paper and see how many questions you can answer.

1 How many carrot cookies can you count?

2 What color is Berry's apron?

3 What is Berry holding?

4 Who else is in the kitchen?

13

Answers on page 47

Playtime!

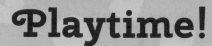

Sultan is the fastest pet in the pawlace. Can you find the speedy words in the wordsearch below? Search down, across, and diagonally.

```
Z  P  B  Y  N  J  R  S
V  R  R  I  V  Q  U  P
W  I  R  D  E  H  N  R
M  A  O  A  A  C  Y  I
G  H  W  F  A  S  T  N
X  S  P  E  E  D  H  T
B  W  W  I  Q  P  J  Y
N  X  X  I  S  U  G  O
```

RUN   **SPEED**

FAST   **SPRINT**

DASH   **GO**

Answers on page 47

Palace Puppy

Pumpkin is a glamorous puppy who loves to play and dance. Can you trace over her name in the space below?

Pumpkin

Now write your name!

My name is

....

15

Natural Napper

Color in this picture of Dreamy taking a catnap.
Use the color code below to help you.

1	**3**
2	**4**

Sweet Petite

Help Petite organize these paw prints by size.
Write 1 for the smallest and 5 for
the largest.

Answers on page 47

Anchors Away!

Treasure is going on an adventure!
Can you match Treasure to her shadow
before she sets sail?

Answer on page 47

Royal Fun

Can you guide Sultan through the maze so he can join Berry and Petite's game?

Start

Finish

Answer on page 48

Draw Sultan

Using the grid as a guide, copy this picture of Sultan onto the next page. Draw one square at a time to make it easier.

Prancing Petite

Petite is speeding off to the racetrack for the Royal Derby. Which two pictures of her are exactly the same?

Answer on page 48

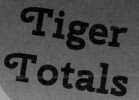
Help Sultan by finishing the math problems below and writing the correct number in each paw print.

Answers on page 48

23

Sweet Sudoku

Each of the pets pictured below should appear once in each row and column. Write the correct letter in the empty boxes to complete the puzzle.

Answers on page 48

Royal Derby Starter

Pumpkin needs a hat for the Royal Derby Starter.
Can you help her design a fun hat for the pony race?

Let your
imagination
run wild!

Complete this puzzle by drawing lines to match the jigsaw pieces to the gaps.

Answers on page 48

Purr-fect Day

Dreamy's purr-fect day involves a lot of napping! How many times can you spot the word SLEEP in the grid below? Search forward, down, and diagonally.

```
S  L  E  E  P  I  W
S  L  D  F  A  T  J
L  S  E  N  X  D  S
E  M  K  E  H  W  L
E  L  V  C  P  S  E
P  A  B  O  H  Q  E
S  L  E  E  P  F  P
```

I can spot SLEEP [   ] times.

Answers on page 48

Cookie Boogie

Treasure has accidentally sprinkled
Berry's cookies with magic glitter and they
have come to life! Design your own
magic cookie here.

Roarsome!

Sultan is ready to play! Use the key below to find out what he is saying.

A C D K N O R

Copy Color

Petite is having a magical day!
Copy the colors to complete the
picture on the opposite page.

Tiara Trouble

Oh, dear—the Palace Pets have mixed their tiaras up! Draw lines to match the tiaras to their owners.

1

a

2

b

3

c

4

d

Answers on page 48

Pretty Patterns

Which picture completes each pattern? Write the correct letter at the end of each row.

a 🐾   b 👑   c ✿   d ❀

1

2

3

4

Answers on page 48

Well, I'll be humdinged! One of these pictures of Ms. Featherbon is different from the others. Can you spot the odd one out?

Answer on page 48

Use this word spiral to discover what Treasure is saying. Cross out every second letter to reveal the answer, then write it in the box below.

The first two letters have been done for you!

A J D P V E E Y N A D H E N R K T U L R N E N A D D H N O T Y D Y

A D _ !

Answer on page 48

Tutu Terrific

Petite loves her friendship tutu.
Color in this sweet picture of her.

Now design your own terrific tutu here! Decorate it with all your favorite things.

Perfect Pirouette

Pumpkin is ready to spin, leap, and twirl. Can you create a backdrop for her special dancing show?

Treasure Trove

Me-wow! How many pairs of starfish has Treasure found? Draw a line to link the matching starfish, then write your answer in the seashell at the bottom of the page.

Answer on page 48

39

Royal Rooms

Each of the pets has their own room that's full of their favorite things. Draw a line to match each of the pets below to the right room. There are clues to help you.

a This room is purr-fect for a sleepy feline.

c This library is terrific for a book-loving pony.

This primp zone is just right for a pampered pup.

This playful pad is roarsome!

Answers on page 48

Berry Sweet

Petite and Dreamy are hungry for cookies!
Help them follow the delicious smell to
reach Berry's freshly baked treats.

A   B   C

Answer on page 48

Royal Cuteness

Sultan just loves to laugh and play! Finish this picture of him with your favorite colors.

Pawfect Pals

Dreamy and Pumpkin are BFFs—Best Friends Fur-ever! Can you spot and circle five differences in the second picture?

Answers on page 48

Splendificent!

Ms. Featherbon loves Cake-tillion, but it sure does get messy! Connect the dots to complete the picture.

Now add your favorite colors.

Answers

Page 3

Pages 4 – 5

Page 7

Page 8
Path c leads to Dreamy's throne.

Page 9
1 = d, 2 = c, 3 = b, 4 = a.

Page 11

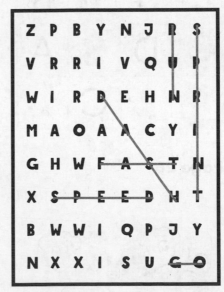

Page 12
5 red, 4 yellow, 2 blue, and 3 purple butterflies.

Page 13
1. There are four carrot cookies.
2. Berry is wearing a pink apron.
3. Berry is holding a pie.
4. Petite is in the kitchen.

Page 14

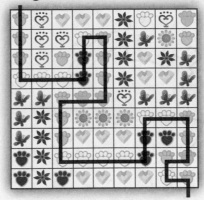

Page 17
4, 3, 5, 2, 1.

Page 18
Shadow 6 is a match

Answers

Page 19

Page 22
1 and 5 are the same.

Page 23
3, 4, 2, 3.

Page 24

Page 26

Page 27

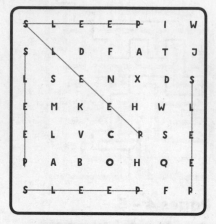

Page 29
ROCK AND ROAR

Page 32
1 = c, 2 = d, 3 = a, 4 = b

Page 33
1 = b, 2 = a, 3 = d, 4 = d

Page 34
4 is the odd one out.

Page 35
ADVENTURE AHOY!

Page 39
There are 5 pairs of seashells.

Pages 40 – 41
a = Dreamy, b = Pumpkin,
c = Petite, d = Sultan.

Page 42
Path c leads to Berry.

Pages 44 – 45